To Jen, Drew, Spence, Dylan, Kate, John, Marrie, Aaron and now . . . Clara! —A.S.

To all of the friends who made me feel special when I was the new kid. —J.J.

Clarion Books is an imprint of HarperCollins Publishers.

Little Blue Truck Makes a Friend

Illustrated in the style of Jill McElmurry by John Joseph

ISBN 978-0-35-872282-3

Typography by Phil Caminiti

22 23 24 25 26 RTLO 10 9 8 7 6 5 4 3 2 1

First Edition

Little Blue Truck Makes a Friend

Alice Schertle

Illustrated in the style of

Jill McElmurry

by John Joseph

Clarion Books

An Imprint of HarperCollins*Publishers*

Horn went "Beep!"
Engine purred.
Friendliest sounds
you ever heard.

Little Blue Truck
was on the road,
taking a drive
with good friend Toad.

Hen came running.
"**Cluck! Cluck! Cluck!**
I've got news!
STOP, Little Blue Truck!

“Someone moved in
down the road—
someone different,
Blue and Toad!”

"**Honk!**" said Goose.
"No feathers, I've heard."
"**Quack!**" said Duck.
"He's a very strange bird!"

“Neigh!” said Horse.
“Does he gallop around?
Do his hooves make a
clippety-cloppety sound?”

"**Moo!**" said Cow.
"What a cow would be doing
is standing around
just quietly chewing."

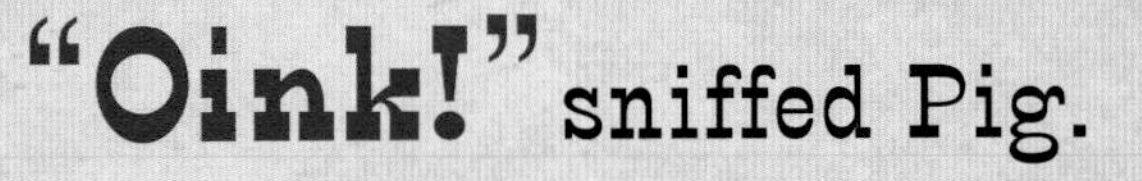

"**Oink!**" sniffed Pig.
"You can see
he can't be a pig
if he's not like me."

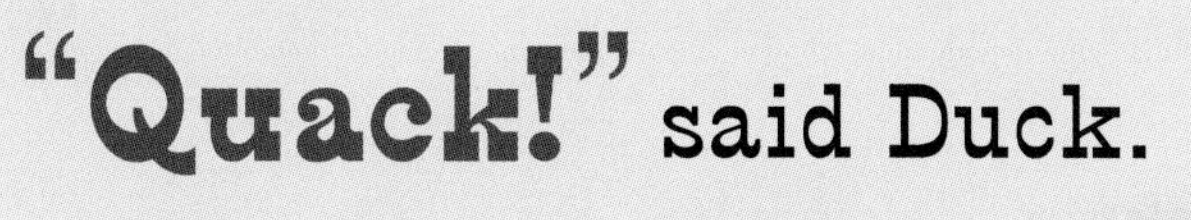

"**Quack!**" said Duck.
"Can he swim? Does he float?"
"**Maaa!** How high
can he jump?" said Goat.

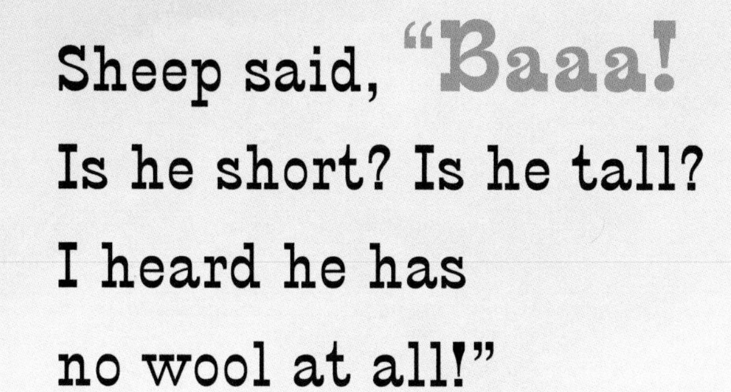

Sheep said, "**Baaa!**
Is he short? Is he tall?
I heard he has
no wool at all!"

"HE'S NOT LIKE ANY ONE OF US!"

"Beep!" said Blue. "What's all the fuss?"

"Somebody new?
Let's go see!
Beep! Who wants
to ride with me?"

They scrambled into
Little Blue Truck,
with a "**Moo!**" and a "**Quack!**"
and a "**Cluck! Cluck! Cluck!**"

"Maaa!" said Goat,
and he jumped in too.
Off they went
with Toad and Blue.

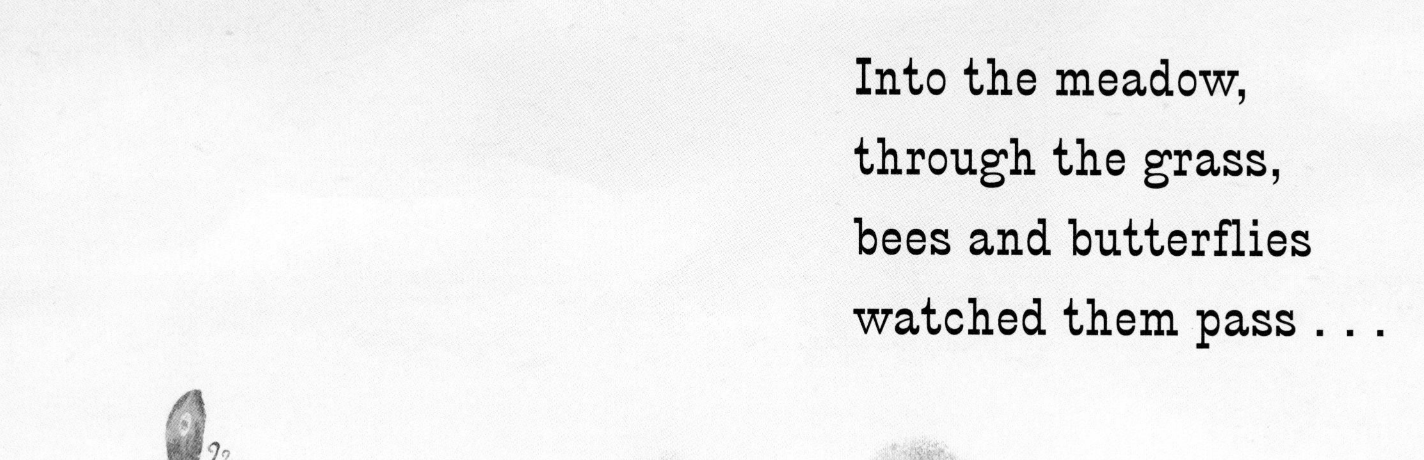

Into the meadow,
through the grass,
bees and butterflies
watched them pass . . .

. . . up a hill
and there they found
a little round door
in a grassy mound.

"Woodchuck's House"
said a sign on the door.
They'd never seen a house
like that before.

HOUSE

"This isn't a coop,
or a barn or a pen—
Cluck! He lives
in a hole!" said Hen.

"Looks cozy to me,"
said Little Blue Truck.

Then . . .
the door swung open
and out stepped Chuck.

"RUN!" honked Goose.
Duck quacked, "HIDE!"
Hen found a pail
and jumped inside.

Goat jumped over
a pile of rocks.

Pig crawled under
some hollyhocks.

Horse leapt over
a low stone wall,
which didn't hide much
of Horse at all.

A tree was all
that Cow could find.
(A lot of Cow
stuck out behind.)

Wherever they hid,
they peeked at Blue
and waited to see
what Chuck would do.

Little Blue's "Beep!" was loud and clear:
"WE ARE VERY GLAD YOU'RE HERE!"

"Croak!" said Toad, and "Beep!" said Blue.
"Just stopped by to welcome you!"

Chuck thumped his feet
on the grassy mound
and whistled, **"Wheee!"**
with a friendly sound.

"I was all alone, and feeling shy.
I sure am glad that you stopped by!
Are there other friends about?"

"**Croak!**" laughed Toad. "COME ON OUT!"

First came Hen,
then Goat and Cow—
"Let's make friends!
Blue showed us how!"

"**Quack!**" said Duck,
and Horse said "**Neigh!**
We didn't need to
run away!"

They gathered round
and Chuck said, "**Wheee!**
More new friends
to visit me!"

"**Beep!**" said Blue.
"Would you like a ride?
We'll show you around
the countryside."

They scrambled into
Little Blue Truck,
and they all made room for
their new friend, Chuck.

Beep! Beep! Beep!